THE
Huckabuck Family

and How They Raised Popcorn in Nebraska
and Quit and Came Back

Carl Sandburg • *Pictures by* **David Small**

FARRAR STRAUS GIROUX • New York

"The Huckabuck Family and How They Raised Popcorn in Nebraska and Quit and Came Back"
from *Rootabaga Stories* by Carl Sandburg, copyright 1923, 1922 by Harcourt Brace & Company
and renewed 1951, 1950 by Carl Sandburg, reprinted by permission of the publisher
Illustrations copyright © 1999 by David Small
Distributed in Canada by Douglas & McIntyre Ltd.
Color separations by Hong Kong Scanner Arts
Printed and bound in the United States of America by Berryville Graphics
Designed by Filomena Tuosto
First edition, 1999. Second printing, 1999

Library of Congress Cataloging-in-Publication Data
Sandburg, Carl, 1878–1967.
    The Huckabuck family and how they raised popcorn in Nebraska and quit and came back /
Carl Sandburg ; pictures by David Small. —1st ed.
        p. cm.
    "The text was originally published in 1923 by Harcourt, Brace & Company
in the book Rootabaga stories by Carl Sandburg."
    Summary: After the popcorn the Huckabucks had raised explodes in a fire
and Pony Pony Huckabuck finds a silver buckle inside a squash, the family decides
it is time for a change.
    ISBN 0-374-33511-7
    [1. Humorous stories.] I. Small, David, 1945– ill. II. Title.
PZ7.S1965Hu 1999
[Fic]—dc21   98-6676

To Sarah

with special thanks to
Alan Benjamin

Jonas Jonas Huckabuck was a farmer in Nebraska with a wife,
Mama Mama Huckabuck, and a daughter, Pony Pony Huckabuck.

"Your father gave you two names the same in front," people had said to him.

And he answered, "Yes, two names are easier to remember. If you call me by my first name Jonas and I don't hear you, then when you call me by my second name Jonas, maybe I will.

"And," he went on, "I call my pony-face girl Pony Pony because if she doesn't hear me the first time, she always does the second."

And so they lived on a farm where they raised popcorn, these three, Jonas Jonas Huckabuck, his wife Mama Mama Huckabuck, and their pony-face daughter Pony Pony Huckabuck.

After they harvested the crop one year, they had the barns, the cribs, the sheds, the shacks, and all the cracks and corners of the farm, all filled with popcorn.

"We came out to Nebraska to raise popcorn," said Jonas Jonas, "and I guess we got nearly enough popcorn this year for the popcorn poppers and all the friends and relations of all the popcorn poppers in these United States."

And this was the year Pony Pony was going to bake her first squash pie all by herself. In one corner of the corncrib, all covered over with popcorn, she had a secret, a big round squash, a fat yellow squash, a rich squash all spotted with spots of gold.

She carried the squash into the kitchen, took a long, sharp, shining knife, and then she cut the squash in the middle till she had two big half squashes. And inside just like outside, it was rich yellow spotted with spots of gold.

And there was a shine of silver. And Pony Pony wondered why silver should be in a squash. She picked and plunged with her fingers till she pulled it out.

"It's a buckle," she said, "a silver buckle, a Chinese silver slipper buckle."

She ran with it to her father and said, "Look what I found when I cut open the golden yellow squash spotted with gold spots—it is a Chinese silver slipper buckle."

"It means our luck is going to change, and we don't know whether it will be good luck or bad luck," said Jonas Jonas to his daughter, Pony Pony Huckabuck.

Then she ran with it to her mother and said, "Look what I found when I cut open the yellow squash spotted with spots of gold—it is a Chinese silver slipper buckle."

"It means our luck is going to change, and we don't know whether it will be good luck or bad luck," said Mama Mama Huckabuck.

And that night a fire started in the barns, cribs, sheds, shacks,
cracks, and corners, where the popcorn harvest was kept. All night long
the popcorn popped.

In the morning the ground all around the farmhouse and the barn
was covered with white popcorn so it looked like a heavy fall of snow.
   All the next day the fire kept on, and the popcorn popped till it was
up to the shoulders of Pony Pony when she tried to walk from the
house to the barn.

And that night in all the barns, cribs, sheds, shacks, cracks, and corners of the farm, the popcorn went on popping.

In the morning when Jonas Jonas Huckabuck looked out of the upstairs window, he saw the popcorn popping and coming higher and higher. It was nearly up to the window.

Before evening and dark of that day, Jonas Jonas Huckabuck, and his wife Mama Mama Huckabuck, and their daughter Pony Pony Huckabuck, all went away from the farm saying, "We came to Nebraska to raise popcorn, but this is too much. We will not come back till the wind blows away the popcorn. We will not come back till we get a sign and a signal."

They went to Oskaloosa, Iowa. And the next year Pony Pony Huckabuck was very proud because when she stood on the sidewalks in the street, she could see her father sitting high on the seat of a coal wagon, driving two big spanking horses hitched with shining brass harness in front of the coal wagon. And though Pony Pony and Jonas Jonas were proud, very proud all that year, there never came a sign, a signal.

The next year again was a proud year, exactly as proud a year as they spent in Oskaloosa. They went to Paducah, Kentucky; to Defiance, Ohio; Peoria, Illinois; Indianapolis, Indiana; Walla Walla, Washington. And in all these places Pony Pony Huckabuck saw her father, Jonas Jonas Huckabuck, standing in rubber boots deep down in a ditch with a shining steel shovel shoveling yellow clay and black mud from down in the ditch high and high up over his shoulders. And though it was a proud year, they got no sign, no signal.

The next year came. It was the proudest of all. This was the year Jonas Jonas Huckabuck and his family lived in Elgin, Illinois, and Jonas Jonas was watchman in a watch factory watching the watches.

"I know where you have been," Mama Mama Huckabuck would say of an evening to Pony Pony Huckabuck. "You have been down to the watch factory watching your father watch the watches."

"Yes," said Pony Pony. "Yes, and this evening when I was watching Father watch the watches in the watch factory, I looked over my left shoulder and I saw a policeman with a star and brass buttons, and he was watching me to see if I was watching Father watch the watches in the watch factory."

It was a proud year. Pony Pony saved her money. Thanksgiving came. Pony Pony said, "I am going to get a squash to make a squash pie." She hunted from one grocery to another; she kept her eyes on the farm wagons coming into Elgin with squashes.

She found what she wanted, the yellow squash spotted with gold spots. She took it home, cut it open, and saw the inside was like the outside, all rich yellow spotted with gold spots.

There was a shine like silver. She picked and plunged with her fingers and pulled and pulled till at last she pulled out the shine of silver.

"It's a sign; it is a signal," she said. "It is a buckle, a slipper buckle, a Chinese silver slipper buckle. It is the mate to the other buckle. Our luck is going to change. Yoo hoo! Yoo hoo!"

She told her father and mother about the buckle. They went back to the farm in Nebraska. The wind by this time had been blowing and blowing for three years, and all the popcorn was blown away.

"Now we are going to be farmers again," said Jonas Jonas Huckabuck to Mama Mama Huckabuck and to Pony Pony Huckabuck. "And we are going to raise cabbages, beets, and turnips; we are going to raise squash, rutabaga, pumpkins, and peppers for pickling. We are going to raise wheat, oats, barley, rye. We are going to raise corn such as Indian corn and kaffir corn—but

we are *not* going to raise any popcorn for the popcorn poppers to be popping."

And the pony-face daughter, Pony Pony Huckabuck, was proud because she had on new black slippers, and around her ankles, holding the slippers on the left foot and the right foot, she had two buckles, silver buckles, Chinese silver slipper buckles. They were mates.

Sometimes on Thanksgiving Day and Christmas and New Year's, she tells her friends to be careful when they open a squash.

"Squashes make your luck change good to bad and bad to good," says Pony Pony.

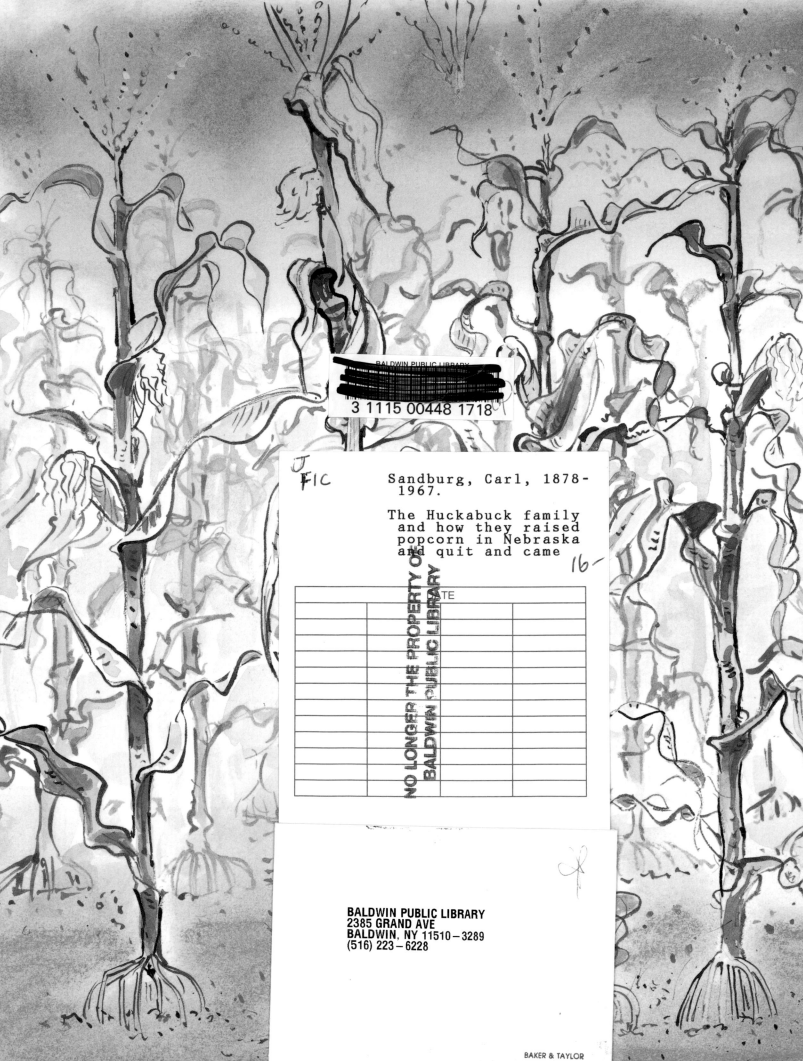